THIS BOOK BELONGS TO

~~Mr. Monkeyjocks~~

THE BEST FAMILY IN THE UNIVERSE

From............................

BLUEY

PENGUIN YOUNG READERS LICENSES
An imprint of Penguin Random House LLC
1745 Broadway, New York, New York 10019

First published in Australia by Puffin Books, 2023

First published in the United States of America by Penguin Young Readers Licenses,
an imprint of Penguin Random House LLC, 2025

This book is based on the TV series *Bluey*.

Visit us online at penguinrandomhouse.com.

Manufactured in China

ISBN 9798217051649 10 9 8 7 6 5 4 3 2 1 HH

The authorized representative in the EU for
product safety and compliance is Penguin Random House Ireland,
Morrison Chambers, 32 Nassau Street, Dublin D02 YH68, Ireland,
https://eu-contact.penguin.ie.

I LOVE MY FAMILY

by Bluey and Bingo

Hi. I'm Bingo and I'm going to tell you why **my family is the best** in the universe.

Our family isn't the best, Bingo.

HUH?!

Muffin's family
is waaay better.

WHAAAT? WHY?

Uncle Stripe buys
Muffin ice cream.

Oh yeah!

When we ask Dad for an ice cream, he just plays Ragdoll.

It's very rude.

And Muffin has an electric car **AND** a pool in her backyard!

Yeah, but the pool's got a crawly thing.

And she's got **LOADS** of Moonlight Unicorns.

And a caravan.

Kids, have you seen the lid
to the water bottle?

It was here this morning . . .

Mum, is Muffin's family better than ours because she has a pool?

A pool doesn't make a family a family.

What makes a family a family, then?

What matters is how much you **LOVE** each other.

How do we know how much we **LOVE** each other?

Well, do we all **LOVE** doing things together?

Yes, I **LOVE** it when Dad plays Café and lets me eat pavlova.

And I **LOVE** beating him at Memory Snap!

We **LOVE** his Duck Cake!

He lets us do his makeup . . .

. . . and say the word **DUNNY!**

We **love** dancing together.

Especially outside.

And making you and Dad
fancy romance dinners.

We **LOVE** playing with our cousins Muffin and Socks, too.

Once, we went backpacking! And we were the backpacks, **He-He**.

I like being pizza sisters with Socks.

And Muffin is a good mechanic.

Sometimes Muffin
gets a bit tired . . .

. . . and we have to look after her.

Who else do you like
spending time with?

Nana!

Everyone gets what they want at Nana's house.

And **GRANDAD!**

He's the best croc catcher.

It was funny teaching him how to use apps.

What about your Aunt
Trixie and Uncle Stripe?

Aunt Trixie was the best
wise old wolfhound.

And Uncle Stripe
loooooves playing
Horsey Ride with us.

Remember when we Faceytalked Muffin and she stole Uncle Stripe's phone?

He-He, that was funny. Uncle Stripe had to chase her all around the house.

But not funny when we saw
Aunt Trixie on the toilet.

Oh dear.

What about Uncle Rad
and Frisky?

We **LOVE** it when
Frisky plays
Torch Mouse.

And Uncle Rad lets us walk on the ceiling!

And we **LOVE** the bedtime stories they tell together.

Who else do we **love** playing with?

Mr. Monkeyjocks!

Forget him! That monkey was too big for his boots.

Hey, Dad! This
is *our* book!

Someone's
jealous.

Well, you can't forget **UNICORSE**.

Oh yes we can!

So, our family is a family because . . .

. . . we play together . . .

. . . we dance together . . .

. . . and we laugh together.

THAT'S why we **LOVE** our family!